# MY SILLY POEMS
# FOR
# KIDS

## ANGELA RIGLEY

*Angela Rigley*

**ISBN-13: 978-1518850783**
**ISBN-10: 1518850782**

Copyright belongs to the author
British Library Cataloguing in Publication
data.

# LULU THE LAMB

Lulu the Lamb is a lively young lamb;
She frolics and gambols all day.
But when she is tired, and she needs to rest,
Sleep just won't come her way.
She wriggles and jiggles, tosses and turns;
Her eyelids will not remain shut.
'Try counting humans,' Mother Ewe says,
'For I heard in the shepherd's hut,
This morning as I was passing by,
That they tell their kids to count sheep,
From anything up to one thousand or more,
When they can't drop off to sleep.'
But try as she may, Lulu wriggles and tosses
Even counts to a thousand and ten;
But then in the morning she jumps up, alert,
And runs out to frolic again.

§§§

# CLARENCE THE CAT

Clarence Calamity,
the clumsy cat
can get into trouble
at the drop of a hat.

He crawls into holes
and cannot get out,
then climbs up tall trees
and down water spouts.

His paws are all pukey;
He's always getting stuck,
but does Clarence bother?
No, for he has good luck.

Now cats should have nine lives;
but Clarence has more.
He must have used twenty;
of that I am sure.

He runs across roads
without looking each way,
and rides on the railways
most of the day.

One day, mark my words,
I am fearful that
good luck will run out
for Clarence the cat.

§§§

# CHARLIE THE PARROT

Charlie the Parrot is twenty-one;
He is so cute and sweet.
He sits on his perch for most of the day,
And doesn't make a tweet.

He wears a little jersey,
Blue-striped - it fits so snug;
It makes you want to squeeze him.
Or give him a great big hug.

His wings are very ragged;
Though once they were so green;
But now they're really tatty,
As you have surely seen.

His dark green head is shiny;
His beak is very yellow.
He catches your attention;
That lovely little fellow.

He sadly was mistreated once;
His feathers all fell out,
But now he lives in comfort;
Of that there is no doubt.

§§§

# CLARICE THE CHAIR ON HOLIDAY

'Now where shall I sit?'
mumbles Clarice the Chair.
'In front of this wall
or perhaps over there?
I liked where I sat
yesterday on the lawn,
so I stayed there all night
'til the onset of dawn.
But I think I'd prefer
to move nearer the flowers,
and sniff the red roses
for a while, maybe hours.
Or shall I divert
to a place by the stream,
where the birdsong will send me
to sleep and to dream?
Must make up my mind,
for I still haven't found
the best spot to park.
I want somewhere that's sound,
perhaps near to the shrubs
where I can keep out of sight,

and no-one will find me
'til later tonight.
I won't have fat bottoms
slouching onto my seat,
or tea spills or coffee
or foul, cheesy feet.
Yes, I think I'll do that,
I'll hide under the trees,
and sway to the swell
of a soft, gentle breeze.
Ah! This is the life.
What a fine peaceful spot.
Oh, no! That bird's plopped on me.
Well, thanks a lot.

§§§

## A JOKE

Have you heard about the couple
who mistook daffodil bulbs for onions?
They both ended up in hospital,
but the doctors say
they should be out by the Spring.

§§§

## SALLY THE SNAIL

So sorrowful and sad
is Sally the Snail,
when she suddenly senses
that she has no tail.

She sobs to her sister,
"Sue, I'm in such a state.
Surely tails are needed
for us snails to walk straight?"

"Oh, Sally, you're silly,"
Big sis Sue starts to yell.
"See over your shoulder.
Your tail's under your shell."

§§§

# TERRY AND FRIENDS

Terry Toad is quite old.
He limps and he squints,
He coughs, never laughs,
Rarely leaves his abode.

His abode is his home,
It's a shoe, nearly new,
Found when he went round
To his friend, Nobs the gnome.

Nobs lives in a tree
Near the wall. He's not tall,
But short, and drinks port.
Nob's best friend is Bet Bee.

Now bees, they might sting,
not Bet Bee, you must see;
Bet's too good, never would,
Never hurt a living thing.

Their enemy is Will;
Oh my gosh, he's a wasp;
He's stripey and stingy
With a barb that could kill.

But Will won't, he's too old.
He coughs, never laughs.
He squints and he limps,
Just like Terry the toad.

§§§

# TILLIE AND TONI

Tillie and Toni are identical twins,
And both look exactly the same;
They each have blue eyes,
And are much the same size,
But, of course, don't have the same name.

Bobby, and Billy, his brother, are twins,
But don't resemble each other at all.
Bobby is fair
With much lighter hair,
Though both of them are really quite tall.

One day Tillie said, "Oh, Bobby, my love,
I really would like us to marry."
"I can't," said young Bob,
Making Till start to sob.
"I love Toni and we must not tarry."

Tillie was sad, for she loved her Bob so;
But Billy, he loved Toni too.
"It's not fair," Tillie said,
And ran off to bed,
While Bill caused a hullabaloo.

Bill ran to his twin, hit Bob on the chin.
"Toni's mine. You can't have her," he said.
So Bobby grabbed Tillie,
And knocked over Billie.
And they both ended up with sore heads.

§§§

# THE LETTER

Muted lapping of water awakens me;
Towards the window I turn my head.
Enticing me, the cool brook babbles past
Over large, rounded stones in its bed.

Out the corner of my eye flashes by
A kingfisher, feathers gleaming blue.
In her mouth is a sprat for her young;
Her feathers reflect the dawn's hue.

Keen to munch on the dewy green grass,
Hops a rabbit; his white tail in view,
To shepherd him back to the burrow,
His mum pops out, right on cue.

Crunch of gravel on path along the side
Announces arrival of man with the post.
Will he have it? If not, woe betide.
That letter that I want the most.

I wait with breath bated for the rattle
Of the letterbox, and then I go.
Is it there, in amongst the junk mail?
Can I spot it? Oh, I really hope so.

With lead boots I go out to the garden,
My whole future depends on this note.
Is kingfisher still there or the rabbit?
I care not as I sit down and gloat.

Hooray, yes I have it. I'm excited.
They've finally offered me the job.
A warden in local nature park;
I'm so happy I think I might sob.

§§§

# ARE WE NEARLY THERE YET?

*Are we nearly there yet?*
a voice comes from behind.

"Not quite, my dear,
wind your window down,
and look at those baby lambs,
frolicking and gambolling
in the field;
the big ones with horns are the rams.
See that colourful pheasant,
its plumage so bright,
and there on the lake is a swan.
You usually love to look at the birds.
Don't tell me, my dear,
that I'm wrong.

*But aren't we nearly there yet?*
*I'm getting bored, you know.*

Just look at the bluebells
spread right through the woods,
clumps of primroses, cowslips there too,
lots of bushes of broom
and sharp, prickly gorse,
hosts of daffodils, yellow in hue.
A waterfall's tumbling down the hill,
droplets sending up vibrant rainbows;
and moss, covering walls and
chopped-off tree stumps,
looks like blotches
of green marshmallows.

*Please say we're nearly there, Mum.*
*How much further is it?*

We've come to the Lakes,
to get our walking boots on;
to be free, to relax and to rest,
away from the hustle and bustle of life,
so please, darling,
stop being a pest.
No, of course, there isn't
a penny arcade,
we are here with not a care;
so stop asking about sea,
and donkeys and sand.
Just breathe in the mountain air.

*But, Mum surely we can't really be there?*
*Oh, it's not fair.*

§§§

## BLUETIT'S REVENGE

Oh, look, there's a bluetit.
It's trying in vain,
to get into my kitchen,
come out of the rain.
So cheekily perched
on the white window ledge,
tip-tapping. Be careful,
you'll fall off the edge.


*Tip-tappety, tappety,*
*let me come through,*
*I can see you inside*
*and I want to join you.*
*There's nothing to stop me,*
*as far as I know,*
*so why can't I get through*
*this dirty window?*

He's pecking away
at the clear window pane,
and peeping inside.
There he goes again.
What on earth can he want
in this old house of mine?
I've no juicy caterpillars
on which he might dine.


*I'll flip-flap my wings,*
*try a different pose,*
*and I might then get in*
*through that stupid window.*
*I'm sure they will like me,*
*without any doubt,*
*but if I can't enter,*
*they'll never find out.*

I'll go fetch my camera,
this sight I must catch,
of a bluetit sat cheeping
on my closed window latch.
Or shall I just open it
and see his intent?
But if I approach,
will he fly off, hell bent?

*Well, I don't understand*
*why I cannot get through.*
*The glass looks okay to me.*
*So I might as well poo*
*all down the silly window,*
*prove I mean business.*
*Ah, now I feel better.*
*Hope they appreciate the mess.*

§§§

## SAMMY THE SPIDER

Sammy the spider is on the alert.
He sits in his web all day long,
Spinning and weaving, repairing the tears,
'Til an unwary fly comes along.

Licking his lips, he charges right out
From his hiding place up in the eave.
He scrambles towards it; it mustn't escape;
He must catch it before it can leave.

He wraps it in silk so sticky and strong;
The poor fly just cannot resist.
Sam gobbles it up; every morsel is gone,
Then he climbs up to wait for the next.

§§§

## DORIS THE DORMOUSE

Doris the dormouse went to sea
In a dingy and dirty dinghy.
She took dishes galore
Of dry slices of boar,
Doris did look a mess,
Draped in a dark, drab dress,
But delighted, she dared to declare,
'I'm the dottiest dormouse out there.'

§§§

# NOT WORKING

Today I won't be working hard,
I can't be bothered to.
My legs are aching, full of pain,
no matter what I do.
Those people there are laughing;
won't someone tell me why?
I'm only going through my act.
If only I could fly!
For then I wouldn't have to walk
on legs that hurt me so,
I'd beat my wings and rise up high,
or flutter way down low.
I'd soar to heights unknown before
and see things never seen
by beast or animal on earth,
go places I've not been.
Oh, wouldn't that be wonderful?
To leave this drudge and toil,
and wander round the world outside
and tread on different soil.
But no, it wouldn't happen so,
I'll never leave this place.

I'm doomed to stay my whole life long,
remain in this rat race.
All right, all right, I'll stand right up
and wave my feet about,
but don't expect a startling show,
I'm sure my toe's got gout.
For a circus elephant just like me
does really have no choice
but do all that he's told to do,
obey his master's voice.


§§§

# A LIMERICK

There once was a lady called Cherry
Who went over to France on a ferry,
Duty free shop on board
Sold the wine she adored,
And she drank way too much and got merry.

§§§

# MOO

I've drunk mugs full of coffee
and cups of tea too,
I've had so much milk
that now I say, 'moo'.
If I am not careful
I'll be chewing the cud,
and rolling round, starkers,
in the dirt and the mud.
My tail will be whisking
to scare off the flies
that get down my ear'oles
and into my eyes.
They'll be calling me Bessie
or Daisy or…Bert?

No, that would be too silly.

§§§

# COMPETITION PAGE

Each day I scan the papers for
the competition page.
If answers somehow I can't get,
then I am filled with rage.

The crosswords are my favourites,
but not the cryptic ones.
I can't tell what on earth they mean,
especially the puns.

My poor dog hates it when I moan
and scratch my perplexed head.
He cries and whines until I stop,
to take him out, instead.

But all the while I'm walking him
my mind is in a whirl.
If only I could get the ten across,
my fists I could unfurl.

I hurry home and grab the pen,
  the seven down I've found.
I've finished it, oh joy of joys,
  I jump and dance around.

But, no, I've not. I'm sorely vexed,
  for when I look again,
the sixteen down's eluded me.
  I have to blame my pen.

It must have run out when I wrote
  the answer to that one.
For sure I can't have missed it,
  so, wherever has it gone?


§§§

# NATURE

Wonderful willows
waving flexible fingers;
ravens raucously roosting;
swallows soaring skyward,
fleetingly flying,
bumblebees busily buzzing;
sweet, succulent strawberries
rapidly ripening;
badgers bravely burrowing;
sparkling sunshine
showering silvery sunbeams;
Nature's naturally nurturing.

§§§

# CLARICE THE CHAIR ON HOLIDAY AGAIN

I'm thrilled to say that we're here again,
and as happy as we can be,
not at the bracing, sandy seashore,
but in mountainous Lake country.

A pleasing change from that fusty old shed
where I usually spend my days,
in the dark and damp, where beetles abound,
and spiders spin webs in the maze.

I'm sitting here with a lovely view
of the gardens, the river and lawn.
In the mornings the clack of woodpeckers
will herald the coming of dawn.

Tomorrow I'll try to squeeze in
between chairs near the barbeque,
on the decking down by the river.
They won't notice me, covered in dew.

She hopes the days will be sunny,

But black clouds o'er yon hills do I see.
I fear she'll be fair disappointed,
for it's raining. Fiddle-de-dee.

The flowers are waving their petals.
They remember me from last year.
Red roses, and orange nasturtiums.
And look, in the woods there's a deer.

Hark, what's that I hear? A joyous jay,
calling to its mate in the trees.
I might even spot a young leveret,
hear the buzzing of bumblebees.

Oh, my goodness, don't you come near me!
Thought that blackbird was going to sit
on my seat, but he'd better not,
for I don't want to be covered in…bits.

Ah, this is the life, think I'll settle here
to relax in the cooling, fresh air,
and enjoy myself same as last year,
in tranquillity, with never a care.
To lap up the mood in the soft breeze,

Cock an ear to the river flowing by.
The rain has passed on, the sun is aglow.
Thank goodness, now I'm quite dry.

I've been here a while now, I love it.
Wonder where she will put me today,
while they go and see sights I've not seen.
But wait. What's that I hear her say?

They're just moving the car, needn't panic.
Phew, thought they were about to go home.
So why are they loading the luggage in,
if they're just going out for a roam?

She's picking me up. Am I going in?
Alas and alack I fear I am.
But I don't want to go back in that car boot.
I want to stay here with the lambs.

Don't take me back to that dark old shed,
to the cobwebs and bugs that I hate.
I want to stay here, in the place I adore.
But will I return? Watch this spa...ce.

## *Author Biography*

*Married to Don, I have 5 children and nine grandchildren, live in Derbyshire, England, and enjoy singing in my church choir, reading, gardening, Scrabble, Sudoku, meals out and family gatherings. The treasurer of my writing club, Eastwood Writers' Group, I am also an Extraordinary Minister of Holy Communion at church, a reader, a flower arranger and a member of the fundraising team for Cafod, my favourite charity.*

I dedicate this book to my children and

grandchildren and to

The Eastwood Writers' Group.

Other books by the author:

Looking for Jamie
A Dilemma for Jamie
School for Jamie
Choices for Jamie
Rewards for Jamie
Florence and the Highwayman
The Peacock Bottle
Nancie
Lea Croft
Harriet of Hare Street
My Book of Silly Poems and Things
*For children:*
Cal the Caveboy
Cal's Good Idea
Cal Saves his Sister
Baarlie the Naughty Lamb
Baarlie Wants to Fly
Baarlie and the Snow
Dotty and Raggy are Lost in the Wood
Dotty is Lost

Reviews of some of my other children's books:
*Nancie a YA set in Victorian Derbyshire*: Fate deals Nancie many hard blows, and Angela takes us on Nancie's journey through a troubled childhood. Nancie takes it all in her stride, without being overly sentimental. Will life ever get better for her? I couldn't wait to find out.This is my favourite Angela Rigley novel.

*Baarlie the Naughty Lamb:* I felt the author, Angela, did a great job, totàlly with the story and images that helps the reader to catch a glimpse of what this ebook story was all about. For these reasons I wish to recommend this ebook for five stars and kids ages 3-8 & anyone who loves to read short cute animal stories. I received this ebook for free and in return, here's my honest review. Great job Angela !

https://www.amazon.co.uk/Angela-Rigley/e/B00607O51M/ref=sr_ntt_srch_lnk_1?qid=1540287989&sr=1-1

Barnes and Noble:

https://www.barnesandnoble.com/s/%22Angela%20Rigley%22?Ntk=P_key_Contributor_List&Ns=P_Sales_Rank&Ntx=mode+matchall

Find me on Twitter: @angierigley; Facebook: Angela Rigley;

LinkedIn;

Instagram: angelarigleyauthor

my website  www.nunkynoo.yolasite.com where you can see lots of pictures of lambs and birds, and some of my Thoughts for the Day that I write for Radio Nottingham;

 myblog: wordpress.com/view/authoryantics.wordpress.com .

Printed in Great Britain
by Amazon

69461607R00026